The Best Kind of Kiss

Margaret Allum

Illustrated by Jonathan Bentley

LITTLE HARE
www.littleharebooks.com

For Imogen – MA

For Ruby and Harvey – JB

Little Hare Books
an imprint of
Hardie Grant Egmont
Ground Floor, Building 1, 658 Church Street
Richmond, VIC 3121, Australia

www.littleharebooks.com

First published 2010
First published in paperback 2010
This edition published 2011

ISBN 978 1 921894 08 4

Cataloguing-in-Publication details are available
from the National Library of Australia

Designed by Vida & Luke Kelly
Additional design by Xou Creative, www.xou.com.au
Produced by Pica Digital, Singapore
Printed through Phoenix Offset
Printed in Shen Zhen, Guangdong Province, China, November 2011

5 4 3 2 1

I like kisses.

I like big kisses ...

and small kisses …

and pecky kisses ...

and smoochy, lip-smacky kisses.

I kiss the cat for a fluffy kiss …

and the dog for a waggly kiss.

I kiss flowers for a petal kiss ...

butterflies for a fluttery kiss ...

dandelions for a whiskery kiss ...

and snowflakes
for a frosty kiss.

before leaving for a sad kiss …

and when arriving
for a hello kiss.

I sometimes like a
smelly-yelly-brother-kiss…

and I often get a rosy-cosy-granny-kiss ...

and I always want a
snuggly-cuddly-mummy-kiss.

But the kiss I love most is a
great, big bristly-growly-daddy-kiss!

That's my favourite kiss of all.